Vanilla Fetish

Chocolate Caramel Vanilla, Volume 2

Shaun J. Phree

Published by PLE Press LLC, 2020.

Also by Shaun J. Phree

Chocolate Caramel Vanilla
Caramel Addiction
Vanilla Fetish
Chocolate Obsession

Nu Nu Lambda
Soror Love

Standalone
No Love Lost: A Poetic Tale
10 Steps to Self Care
Her Mother, My Love
Never
Writer's Surge
Classified

Table of Contents

CHAPTER ONE 1
CHAPTER TWO 5
CHAPTER THREE 13
CHAPTER FOUR 19
CHAPTER FIVE 27
CHAPTER SIX 31
CHAPTER SEVEN 39
CHAPTER EIGHT 45
CHAPTER NINE 49
CHAPTER TEN 55
CHAPTER ELEVEN 61
EPILOGUE 63

CHAPTER ONE

"I love you, Ashli, baby." Brian held Ashli close to him by her waist. He could smell the strawberry in her hair. He was intoxicated with her. He pulled her in for a kiss, but she resisted. *Is she not into me?*

"Brian, I really like you, and I could see myself growing deeper feelings for you…" Ashli said. Brian felt a lump in his chest rising to his throat. He invited Ashli to meet his family so they could move to the next stage in their relationship. *Here we stand in the middle of this five-star hotel suite I booked for our special weekend, and she doesn't love me.* "…I'm just not there yet, baby."

"That's ok. Ashli, I don't want you to say anything that isn't true. Take your time. We will slow down," he responded.

"Ugh! Thank you!" Ashli jumped into Brian's arms with a sigh of relief. He held her as close as he could.

"I still love you," he whispered into her ear. Ashli nuzzled her face into his neck and sighed again.

"OK, OK. That's enough with all this mushy stuff. Can we go now?" Ashli asked. Brian was stubborn about Ashli meeting his family. He told her they couldn't move forward without it.

"Absolutely, madam," Brian held out his arm for Ashli. She smiled at him and wrapped her arm in his. The two were headed to the hotel lobby to meet with Brian's little sister and ride together to his mother's house.

"HELLO, MA'AM, MY NAME is Ashli Jameson; nice to meet you," Ashli greeted Brian's mother. Her phone vibrated in her pocket, but this wasn't a good time to check it. On the ride over, Brian's sister gave her a rundown of their parents; cell phone interruptions were a pet peeve.

"I'm glad to finally meet you, Ashli. Brian can't stop talking about you. She is as beautiful as you said, Brian." Brian's mother said politely. "Call me Agatha...none of that, ma'am or Mrs. Schultz. Ok?"

"Yes, ma'...Agatha," Ashli laughed. "You have a beautiful home."

"Thank you, Ashli. We raised Brian and his sisters here," she responded, pride on her face as she reviewed their home.

"One day, I hope to raise my kids here..." Brian waited for a response from

Ashli, but she only smiled at him. "Ashli, this is my father, Robert Schultz."

"Nice to meet you, Mr. Schultz." Ashli shook his hand lightly.

"Nice to finally meet you too, Ashli." Robert smiled and cradled her hand in his. She pulled back. Brian softly touched Ashli's shoulder to get her attention.

"Do you want a drink of wine?" he asked her.

"A glass of white wine, please," Ashli responded. Her phone started vibrating again. She ignored it, but everyone else didn't.

"Sweetheart, are you going to let your phone keep vibrating?" Robert asked.

"It's not important right now," Ashli answered.

"It's better if you check it now than to wait for it to go off during dinner when it would be an interruption. Don't you agree?" Brian's father hinted.

Ashli took the hint and smiled.

"I will be right back," Ashli excused herself. She pulled out her phone and saw four missed calls, two missed facetimes, and eight text messages. All the notifications from Kevin, her husband. Ashli told him she was going on a girl's trip and wouldn't be able to answer her phone, but it didn't stop him from trying. Ashli looked around to make sure no one was following her, and she went outside to the front porch. She found a secluded corner and called Kevin back.

"Hello," he answered.

"Hey, is something wrong?" Ashli asked.

"No, nothing's wrong. I just missed you. Why didn't you Facetime me? I want to see your gorgeous face." Kevin questioned.

"I told you I can't talk like that during this trip, baby. The girls would kill me if they knew I had to sneak off to talk to you." Ashli lied.

"They are just mad their husbands and boyfriends don't love them like I love you," Kevin said.

"I am so lucky. Ok, I have to go. I will try to call you tonight, ok?" Ashli asked. Brian was inside searching for Ashli when his father told him she was outside returning a call.

"OK, I will talk to you later, baby. I love you." Kevin said. Before Ashli could respond, Brian opened the front door. He startled her; she immediately put the phone on mute.

"I will be right in, baby; I'm getting off the phone now," Ashli said to stop Brian in his tracks.

"Ok, baby, I will put your glass on the table," Brian responded.

"Thank you so much," Ashli said. She waited until she heard the front door close. She hurried to unmute the phone, "Kevin?"

"What happened? I didn't hear anything?" Kevin responded with confusion.

"My cheek muted the phone. I was sitting here talking, and you couldn't hear anything," Ashli quickly responded. "Anyway, I love you. I will talk to you soon."

"Ok, baby. Have fun." Kevin hung up. Brian slowly backed away from the other side of the front door. Brian's father noticed the uneasy look on Brian's face but didn't think it was the right time to inquire about it. Brian sat the wine glass on the table and sat down just as Ashli entered the house.

"I'm so sorry for the interruption. My friends can't seem to live without me." Ashli lied.

"I know the feeling," Brian stood up and hugged Ashli. He felt the agitation pulsing through her body; he held her tighter until she relaxed.

CHAPTER TWO

Brian beat the sunrise the next morning. He wrote a sweet, loving note on the hotel stationary to let Ashli know he was running out to run a couple of errands for his mother and would return soon. He neatly folded and propped it next to a single rose on the nightstand.

The cool air conditioning ran down his back in the elevator. It calmed his jittery nerves. He wiped his sweaty palms on his jeans before exiting the elevator.

"Good morning. Can you check to see if my car is here yet? I'm Mr. Schultz," Brian asked the front desk attendant.

"One moment," a heavy-set, pale-skinned woman with red hair responded. The tension fell from Brian's body, even if only for a moment when he leaned against the front desk. His heart finally slowed down and started beating at a normal pace. "Yes, Mr. Schultz, your driver is waiting for you outside."

"Thank you, ma'am." Brian nervously rubbed his hands together, trying to discourage sweating. It didn't help.

"IS THIS WHAT YOU'RE looking for?" a young, feminine, blonde salesman asked as he leaned towards Brian with a two-carat diamond engagement ring.

"Yeah, that's it." Brian daydreamed about Ashli's face lighting up with joy when she saw the ring. "It's perfect."

"Look at you all in love. I hope she deserves that longing stare into space." The salesman envied Ashli.

"She is. She is worth way more, but this is the best I can do." Brian smiled as he handed over his credit card.

"Trust me, honey, this ring is more than enough." He softly placed the ring in a velvet box. "See you in five years for an upgrade."

"Thank you...wait...5 years?" Brian questioned as he glanced at his name tag. "Why five years, Kasey?"

"Baby, you will need to upgrade that ring every five years; keep her happy and staring at it." Kasey responded while handing Brian his bag. "Good luck."

Brian gripped the bag as it slipped around in his sweaty hands. The thought of taking such a major step with Ashli scared the shit out of him but also made him feel like he was floating.

"WAKEY, WAKEY, SLEEPY head," Brian kissed Ashli all over her face as she giggled."

"I'm already awake, crazy," she responded. "Where did you go? I missed you."

"Did you get my note?" Brian scanned the room. "I ran an errand."

"What type of errand? Details, baby, details." Ashli sat up smiling. She had a feeling the errand was a gift for her.

"None of your business, nosey rosey." Brian laughed.

"You are so corny. Move so I can get in the shower," Ashli pushed her slightly bronze, naked body past Brian, jumped up, and headed towards the bathroom. She paused, leaning on the bathroom door, and looked over her shoulder at Brian. "It would be a shame to shower alone, especially after I had to wake up alone."

"Oh, so you want some company. I think I can help with that." Brian swept Ashli into his arms, kissing her intensely, walking to the shower from memory.

Brian slowly lowered Ashli to the ground before beginning to remove his shirt.

"No, sir." Ashli jumped into his arms and straddled him. "We will take your clothes off, but you won't put me down." She locked her legs around his waist and started pulling off his shirt. He could feel her leg grip loosening; he quickly caught her by her ass. She kissed him with gratitude. She reached below his hands and started unbuttoning his pants. He lowered her to allow her to feel him growing. She was already wet, but that made her flinch between her thighs. She hurried to unzip his pants and release the grip on his waist; they fell to the ground. He stood in his boxers with his pants around his ankles; they indulged in each other, kissing like a drug addict finally getting their hit. They wanted to move to the shower together but couldn't disconnect. It was too late. His dick freed itself from his boxers and was dancing just below Ashli; she could feel him teasing her. She guided him into her as she gasped for air.

"Oh, My, Go..." Ashli's words quickly turned into mumbles and moans. Brian slowly raised and lowered Ashli, knowing she wanted him to increase his speed. She locked her legs around his waist, attempting to force him to move faster with no luck. The intensity was building inside her; she bit into his shoulder and neck and dug her fingernails into his back. She lost control and wrapped her arms and legs around his body, buried her face in his neck; shivering and shaking, she came. Her body collapsed in his arms. Before he could keep going, she quickly jumped off him, pushed him to the bathroom floor, and remounted him. This time she was in control. She rode him until she felt him pulsating inside her. *No condom. Damn it.* His body collapsed on the floor. He reached for her to lay on him, but she wasn't there anymore.

"Did you put on a condom?" Ashli was searching the floor and checking between her legs.

"No, when did I have time to put on a condom?" Brian responded calmly as his pale body lay on the bathroom floor amongst his clothes.

"Fuck, fuck, fuck." Ashli panicked. She snatched a face towel off the shelf and started the shower.

"What are you doing?" Brian was confused. *Did it matter? They were spending their life together.*

"We have to go to the store. The morning after pill." She stated. She didn't bother to look at him. She checked the temperature of the shower and jumped in. He could see her attempting to wash his seed from between her legs, hoping it would somehow just come out as she squatted in the shower. He picked up his clothes and walked out the bathroom, closing the door behind him. *Would it be so bad to have a baby with him?*

THE ENTIRE RIDE TO the pharmacy was quiet. Ashli sat close to her door and, as far as possible, from Brian. He noticed her behavior and attempted to soothe her. Nothing worked. She told him to stay in the car while she went into the pharmacy. He wanted to be with her. She didn't. He sat in continued silence without her for ten minutes. When she returned, she said it was done. The ride back to the hotel was a bit different.

"I was scared. I'm sorry. I freaked out. I'm not ready to be a mom yet." She confessed to him, explaining why she was so cold towards him.

"All you have to do is talk to me. I would never leave you to deal with anything on your own." Brian could see the tears building in Ashli's eyes. "I'm always here for you."

"I know Brian. It's just so hard for me. Be patient with me, please?" Ashli slid her hand into Brian's hand, squeezing with anticipation.

"Ashli, can you see yourself with me? Getting married? Having kids?" Brian asked as he pulled into a parking space at their hotel. He turned off the car and turned to Ashli to give her his full attention. Her hand still in his, he reassured her, "I know we are slowing down. If you can't see the possibility, I'm not sure what I'm doing."

Ashli knew her reaction to their slip-up was going to cost her, but she didn't expect him to go into a full relationship conversation. Kevin was at home waiting for her to return. She looked down at her ring finger, which was missing her wedding ring, intentionally. Kevin gave her security financially. Brian gave her the attention she craved. She couldn't let either go.

"Brian, I can see myself growing old with you and everything that comes along with it. I just need time to get to where you are. Please don't stop loving me. I care for you so much." Ashli held her breath, waiting for Brian's response. She couldn't lose him.

"I could never stop loving you, Ashli. You are my heart. I know there's more going on in that head of yours. I hope you feel comfortable sharing it with me...soon." Brian looked Ashli in the eyes. She could feel the intensity of his stare. *He knew something. But what.*

"I don't deserve you." Ashli leaned over into the driver's seat, wrapping her arms around Brian's neck, waiting for his arms to settle around her waist. One hand on her back, weakly pulling her in. She pulled back. The look on his face was concerning. Her phone rang.

"Are you going to answer it?" Brian stared at her phone and then into her eyes. "Nothing is more important than you are right now." Ashli reached into her pocket and silenced her phone without pulling it out. She couldn't let him see the name displayed. There was a good chance it would be Kevin. When the phone stopped vibrating in her pocket, she pulled it out and put it on Do Not Disturb. Turned it to face Brian so he could see. Luckily, she turned it back around because as soon as she did, Kevin's face popped up on Facetime. *Do Not Disturb.* "See, now it's on do not disturb, so nothing can interrupt us."

Brian leaned over and kissed Ashli with her face cupped in his hand. He opened the driver's door.

"We should start getting ready. My mom is expecting us soon." Brian got out of the car and headed towards the hotel without Ashli. She didn't move. Testing him to see how long he would walk without her. He stopped halfway through the parking lot, turned around, and waved her to come on. She took her time getting out the car and walking towards him. He swept her into his arms with a hug. It made her feel better. It made her feel loved. *Why was he acting like that?*

CHAPTER THREE

"Ashli, babe, give me a call when you get this." Kevin left another message for his wife. *Where is she?* His phone rang.

"Hey baby, I'm here. Where are you? Oh wait, I see you." Kevin saw his wife waving in the distance, and a smile spread quickly across his face. He enjoyed his time without her, but real life was inevitable. She dropped her carry-on and ran towards him. He opened his arms, welcoming her in. "I missed you so much, My Baby!"

"I missed you. How was your trip? How are the ladies?" He didn't speak to her much during this trip, which was unusual.

"It was crazy. I need a break from them for a while." Ashli laughed at her own comment. *She really doesn't answer questions.* "They are doing well, and they all said hi. You know they love you."

"You love them, so I love them, babe. I'm so glad to see you." Kevin lied. He was enjoying his time away from his wife. It made him feel like he was single again. He enjoyed the weekend with two beautiful women.

"So, what did you do while I was gone?" Ashli asked.

"I worked as always. You know I have to keep them credit card bills paid." Kevin joked. He remembered the $2500 he had just paid out this weekend for her credit cards. She was lucky he was comfortable spending this type of money on her.

"Well, if it's the only way you can show me you love me...maybe I should charge more." Ashli laughed and playfully slapped Kevin's face. He grabbed her wrist mid-slap and pulled her in close to him.

"Don't play like that." Their joking manner quickly turned serious. Ashli snatched her wrist away.

"Don't grab me like that. I told you about that. I'm not your kid." Ashli sighed as she walked away. "Didn't take long, did it."

The car ride home was full of noise, car horns, people yelling, music playing... but nothing else from Ashli. The air conditioning was no match for her icy demeanor. It was almost 100 degrees outside, and she could frost the windows. Her attention remained on her cell phone, scrolling through social media posts, and deliberately not looking at Kevin. To be honest, he didn't care. He connected his phone to the car's Bluetooth and played his favorite playlist.

"I'm hungry. Take me to Sweeties. I want some soul food." Ashli demanded. Kevin pulled up Sweeties on his navigation; it was on their way.

He put his phone down and acted as if she didn't make her demand.

"Please? I am really hungry, baby. Are you going to let me go hungry?"

Ashli whined to get her way, and usually, it worked. Kevin wasn't affectionate, and he realized he would have to pay for that...literally. He made sure Ashli was comfortable and didn't need or want anything. She still complained too much for him, but he just ignored her.

"It's on the way; call and put in an order, and I'll stop." Kevin didn't even look at Ashli. Whatever she wanted, she got.

"Thank you." Ashli rolled her eyes, thinking he wouldn't see her. He did. He wondered why she had such disdain for him. She pulled out her phone, quickly running through her order with the cashier on the other end. She held her hand out to him, signaling him for his card. She didn't take a moment to look at him, smile at him, something. He pulled his card out of his pocket and handed it to her. "Ok, here's the card number..."

By the time they made it home, Ashli convinced Kevin to make two more stops after picking up their food. She complained about needing new clothes for work. Ashli worked in a spa and was pursuing her cosmetology degree. She waxed everything on the body that could be waxed. She worked a lot when she was in town, and any spare time went towards shopping and studying.

Ashli quickly emptied her arms when she entered their home, dropping her shopping bags on the couch before opening her phone. A little person came running down the hallway; she just dodged the kid and kept walking. Turning her attention to the newest posts and comments, he could hear her long nails tapping on the screen of her phone. Kevin sat the food in the kitchen just in time for his arms to open to the brightest star in his life...his baby boy, Kevin Jr. The sound of their bedroom door slamming echoed through the house. He turned his attention to his son.

"Boy, what have you been up to?" Kevin thanked the nanny as she walked into the living room, collecting her things. He ripped a check out of his checkbook. "Here's the week's total, and thank you so much for staying a bit longer today. I added a little extra for your flexibility."

"There's no need, Kevin, but thank you as always." She swung her shawl over her slim shoulders, and the ends landed on her curvaceous hips and ass. He licked his lips, lingering too long on her black leggings, hugging her thickness. When his eyes finally landed on hers, she smiled at him. "If you like what you see, do something about it."

Kevin's dick started growing, he stepped towards her. Her sheer shawl covered the loose-fitting crop top, lightly dancing with her honey-colored D cups. She stood waiting with one eyebrow raised, doubting his bravery. His wife was just in the other room. He didn't care. His son was sitting in the corner playing. He did care. "Jas, meet me. 11:30 tonight."

"I knew you didn't have it in you. I will see you later." She walked over to the little bronze boy playing and kissed him on the forehead. "I will see you later, little guy."

Kevin watched Jas walk to her car. He replayed his weekend in his mind.

He, Jas, and Kevin Jr. spent the weekend together, like a family. KJ loved Jas, and she lit up with love for KJ. Kevin thought about their one-on-one moments in the shower, on the couch, on the kitchen counter, and in the guest room where they slept together each night. He watched as his heart swayed down the sidewalk, away from him. He was yanked from his real-life fantasy to his reality.

"Bring me some popcorn, please, babe," Ashli yelled from the bedroom. He stood in the doorway, stalling as he watched her drive away. *11:30 couldn't come soon enough.* He grabbed the bag of popcorn on the way to their bedroom.

"Here you are, baby. What are you up to?" He sat on the bed.

"Mmmhmph, just online. I didn't want to interrupt what you were doing, I just wanted some popcorn. Thanks." She patted him on the back and gave him a soft push. Then waved. She wanted him to leave. She was gone for a long weekend and she didn't even want to spend time with him when she returned. *11:30, hurry up.*

"Alright, I'm going in the living room with KJ. Want to spend some time with him?" Kevin knew the answer.

"Of course, I do. As soon as I'm done with this, I will be right there." Ashli didn't bother to look up at Kevin while she lied. She just motioned towards her phone and then waved at him again.

"You don't really seem interested in spending time with our son." He didn't want to argue with her, but he knew he had to slip out the door at 11. The only way that was happening was if she was mad at him. KJ was always a dependable subject.

"First, I'm so tired of having the argument with you. You wanted YOUR kid, and now you have him. Second...I love him, but he is not my kid. He is the product of your affair. You're lucky I didn't just leave your ass then. Shit, be happy I stayed and take care of him and you." Ashli froze with a look of daring. Daring Kevin to respond in any way that was against what she was saying.

"I'm going to take KJ to my mom's for a while. She called for him a few times this weekend." Kevin pulled his computer bag off the floor and stuffed his laptop inside.

"Now you're going to leave and not come back all night. Like I don't know what's really going on there." Ashli raised her voice.

"I'm not arguing with you. Not with KJ here. You know how I feel about that." Kevin glared at Ashli. She backed down.

"I hope you enjoy your evening Kevin. You might want to take a shower before you see her, you smell like outside." Kevin pulled a few things out of his dresser and tossed them into a duffel bag. He leaned forward as Ashli slowly pushed past him. As if she did not have enough room to walk out of the room. "Bye, Kevin. I come home, and less than two hours later, you are running to her. Bye Kevin"

"I'm going to my mother's." She rolled her eyes at him when he walked into the living room. He watched her scrolling through her phone quickly. The tapping of her nails against her screen sounded like Morse code. *No need to pay any more attention to her. She was lost in her world.* He picked up his son, the diaper bag, and his keys. "I'll be back tomorrow."

"I really don't care anymore Kevin. Tell your mother I said hi when you drop KJ off." She dropped her phone on the couch and went to hug KJ.

"Bye, baby boy. I will see you tomorrow. Have fun with your granny."

She didn't bother to say anything else to Kevin. She sat back on the couch and picked up her phone. He paused for a moment, *why was he still with her?* He silently left the house.

CHAPTER FOUR

KJ was settled in his booster seat, dancing to his favorite kid's video he watched on his tablet. Kevin loved his son. He was the greatest gift and came from a mistake. Kevin struggled with fidelity until KJ. Ashli was sure he would never be faithful to her. Three years ago, one of Kevin's flings turned into the largest earthquake in their marriage and the birth of his son. He was sure Ashli would leave him, but when she didn't, he promised to stay faithful as long as they had a marriage to fight for. KJ's mom couldn't take care of him, and their part-time arrangement turned into full custody. Ashli went from a comfortable housewife to a working mother without having a baby, and she wasn't happy about it. Over the years, her resentment grew, and it showed.

"Looks like we are here, KJ. Ready to see granny?" Kevin pulled into his mother's driveway.

"Yes, Daddy." KJ bounced in excitement.

"Alright, lil man, let's go." Kevin pulled KJ and his things out of the car. His mother stood at the screen door with a huge smile on her face. "Hey, ma."

"Hey, baby." She kissed Kevin on the cheek. "There's granny's big boy."

KJ jumped into his granny's arms, laughing as she planted kisses all over his face. Their relationship was strong; it had a lot to do with KJ spending most of his first year living with his granny. KJ's mother dropped him off with her frequently without telling Kevin. She knew KJ was a heavy weight on their marriage; as a woman, she understood.

"I'll pick him up tomorrow afternoon." Kevin kissed his mom and hugged his son.

"Going to see her." Kevin paused. He didn't want to turn around and face his mother. "Why are you doing this? You know I don't like it, but just divorce her baby."

"Ma, you know I can't do that right now. Not until she graduates. I did this to us. It doesn't make anything ok, but I owe her to at least get her through school. You know I'm paying for it."

"You can write that into the divorce agreement." KJ ran into his room minutes before. Kevin stared into his mother's concerned eyes as she held his face in her hands. "You deserve to be happy, even after you make big mistakes. When are you going to stop punishing yourself? Better yet, when are you going to stop letting her punish you?"

"I love you, ma. I will see you tomorrow." He ignored her questions, kissed her on the cheek again, and headed towards his car.

"Tell Jas I said hello." She glared at him when he quickly turned around. "I'm not stupid, boy. If a man is happy like that and his wife has nothing to do with it, another woman does. And I haven't done anything, so what other woman is there?"

His mother left him standing in her driveway. Kevin picked his lips off the ground and got into his car. She read his situation in just a few minutes. He shook off her words and called Jas.

"Well, hello there, stranger. And to what do I owe this pleasure?" Jas teased him on the other end of his phone.

"You owe it to yourself. I can't get enough of you. Meet me at our spot at 11:30," Kevin said.

"Yet not enough to actually be with me. I will see you there. I can't wait to be in your arms," she responded. She hung up immediately. He texted her a short poem expressing his desire and adoration for her. She responded with heart emojis and *then man up and make me yours.*

KNOCKING AT THE DOOR signaled the start of his night. It was her. The night was theirs. He opened the door, and she slapped him. He stepped back with caution.

"That's for making me have to meet you at a hotel room." Jas pushed past him into the suite. He snatched her up by her forearm and held her close to him.

"Touch my face again, and it better be in an affectionate manner," he softly threatened her. She yanked her arm back from him, rolled her eyes, and tossed her bag on the couch. "Now get your ass in the shower and hurry it up."

"No," Jas refused verbally but complied as always. She knew better than to completely refuse his request. Money held his marriage with Ashli together, but Jas didn't care about his money. She cared about him, the man. He was incredible when he was allowed to be himself. He had more going on in his head than most people thought. "What's wrong?"

Jas could read the stress on Kevin's face. Something was bothering him, and she wouldn't move until she knew he was okay.

"Nothing..." Kevin lied. Jas walked over to Kevin as he sat on the bed. Her halter-styled sun dress flowed around her as she moved. She lifted his head with one finger and met his eyes with hers. She asked again with her eyes. "It's nothing I want to ruin our night with. I'm just, tired. I've never experienced a woman who would spend her life punishing me rather than giving me a divorce and living her best life."

"Kevin, she feels you owe her a forever life in comfort and love. It doesn't matter if she changed, fell in love with other people, or is being deceptive. All she can see is your mistakes...what she isn't getting from you. All she can see is you pushed her there." Jas explained.

"I will give her whatever she wants in the divorce. I just have to be ok to take care of my son. That's all." Kevin hung his head. Jas picked his face back up and looked into his eyes again. "She wants to suck me dry."

"It doesn't matter what anger and hurt she still feels. This is about you and your son. Do what's best for you two. Everyone else will fall into place if they are meant to stay, baby." Jas reassured him. He gave her a half smile; he knew her intentions were pure. Not many women would help a man understand his wife before sleeping with him. "Right now, it is about you."

Jas stepped back and pulled Kevin to stand up. She motioned him to trade places with her, and she stood in front of the bed he was just sulking on. She reached up, behind her neck and untied her dress. It slowly draped around her curves as the dress fell to the bed and slid to the floor, leaving her standing in just her strapless bra. She released her voluptuous breasts from her bra. Kevin was speechless. Her body was perfect. She sat on the bed and seductively opened her legs. Kevin fell to his knees in front of her, aroused by the sugar dripping down her freshly shaven lips. He kissed her soft thick thighs and trailed to the sugar between her legs. She closed her eyes, fell back onto the bed, and lost herself. Kevin fed on her like a dehydrated vampire. She wrapped her legs around his neck and rode his face to multiple orgasms. He fell back on the floor like a fat kid after a Sunday dinner buffet with her sugar glaze dripping from his chin. Jas attempted to sit up only to see the smile on Kevin's face; mission accomplished. The growth in his pants was much more interesting to her.

"I want him." She stated, gathered her energy and crawled to him after sliding off the bed. "I want you." She opened his jeans and released her target. "I want you inside me."

"Jas, baby, wait." Kevin reluctantly protested. He didn't want to stop but knew he didn't have a condom on. She wrapped her legs around his waist and muffled his words with her kisses. Before he could say anything else, Jas slid him inside her, and he lost himself. "Fuck!"

Jas knew Kevin was in love with her even if he couldn't say it. It was bad enough they were sleeping together while he was married; he knew he couldn't commit to anyone else. He also couldn't stop seeing Jas. Even the sweat off her neck tasted sweet to him; he was in trouble. After 20 minutes, the two went limp on the floor. He knew he had come inside her. She did too. Neither of them said anything about it. They gathered themselves and fell into bed. Their plans for the evening weren't going to happen. They spent the night wrapped in each other's arms, talking, making love, and eating. The sun was their reminder to get a couple of hours of sleep before checking out. If only they could live like this every day.

"GOOD MORNING." JAS kissed Kevin's stubbled chin to wake him. "We have to get ready to go soon."

Kevin didn't open his eyes, rejecting the idea of getting up. "Late checkout"

"You could have told me." Jas punched him in the ribs. "Have me up when I don't have to be."

"I didn't set it up yet. I will pay the extra fee. I'll set it up right now on my phone." Kevin could feel Jas staring at him since he hadn't opened his eyes yet. "Fine, I'm up."

Kevin grabbed his phone, swiped across the screen for a few minutes, then laid back down.

"Well?" Jas waited for an answer.

"I just booked the room for another night. We can leave whenever we're ready." Kevin laid back down and dramatically closed his eyes, making sure Jas saw him.

"Are we staying another night?" She knew she was pushing it.

"You know I can't do that. It's me and you for as long as we can today." Kevin responded. He was hurt by the disappointment on her face.

"Jasmyne, it's me and you. I just need a little more time."

"I know, baby. I'm there every day. I know." Jas knew he was being honest with her. She could see his love for her in his eyes and the sincerity in his touch. It didn't make the pain in her heart hurt any less. She cuddled into his arms and closed her eyes to dream of their life together. They fell back to sleep, together.

CHAPTER FIVE

Ashli sat in silence until she heard Kevin's car pull out of the driveway. She was free. She opened her phone to find her favorite playlist. Kevin would be gone for the night and into tomorrow. She pressed play, and the music echoed through the house.

"Time to have some fun," she said to herself. She undressed until she was wearing nothing but her matching bra and panties. She took seductive photos on the couch. She texted a few of the photos to Brian and waited for a response. "That should do it."

Ashli didn't know what she was doing with Brian or what path her marriage would take. Honestly, she didn't care. Ashli was more concerned with herself than any of the relationships she was in. There was one, she couldn't stand but couldn't get enough of, Persia. She met Persia a while back when she was hanging with her stud best friend all the time. Persia thought Ashli was gay, and she never corrected her. The truth is that Ashli hadn't been with another girl since she was 16. It was all about the sex then, and it was all about the sex now with Persia. It was the best sex she had ever had in her life. She was really craving a fix. She texted two pics to Persia with three words... *Where are you?* Less than a minute later, her phone rang.

"Hello," Ashli answered her phone.

"What time?" Persia asked.

"Midnight. My place. Use your key. I don't feel like talking." Ashli said softly.

"Midnight on the dot. See you then." Persia hung up the phone.

Ashli and Persia didn't have an emotional connection, but the sexual chemistry was undeniable. Persia was polyamorous and didn't mind their relationship revolving around sex. She knew about Kevin, but Ashli lied about Kevin knowing about Persia. She told Persia they didn't speak about her interactions with females. It wasn't the first time Persia had a relationship with a married woman; it was common. It didn't matter either way. They agreed to act like coworkers if they ever crossed each other's path in public. She jumped into the shower, touched up her body hair maintenance, and got dressed.

THE SPARE BEDROOM WAS illuminated by tiny candles. The music played too low to understand the lyrics but loud enough for the couple not to care. Freshly washed Egyptian cotton sheets and a white duvet were pulled back invitingly. The air was sweet, like strawberries. Persia entered the dark house with only the light from her cell phone. She walked directly into the spare bedroom. The only room in the house she'd ever spent time in. Ashli entered the bedroom from the bathroom. She stood in all-white lace, barely covering her breasts and completely open between her legs. Her French-tipped toes were bare on the carpet. Her skin shimmered under the candlelight. It was the only time Persia could see the ridiculously small bit of African American blood running through Ashli's veins.

"I started without you. I couldn't wait." Ashli's French tip nail dangled between teeth teasing her full pink lips. The other hand traced a blade across her neck down to her breasts. "Now I'm irritated. I'm still waiting."

"Shut the fuck up!" Persia raised her voice. She snatched the blade from

Ashli's hand. "Midnight. We said midnight. You never listen, do you."

The blade scratched across the lace piercing the skin on Ashli's neck. A few red drops invaded the pure white lace. Ashli exhaled. The blade was still pressed against her skin. She rocked back and forth, creating more friction between her thighs.

"Stop." Persia shoved her hand between Ashli's clinching legs. She grabbed

Ashli and held her. "You disgust me."

Persia wrapped her fingers around Ashli's neck and tossed her to the bed. She used the blade to violently cut the lace from Ashli's body, leaving small cuts. Ashli lay naked and shaking on the bed.

"Open your legs." Persia directed but Ashli hesitated. Persia grabbed Ashli's thigh purposely digging her fingers into her flesh. Ashli flinched and opened her legs. "You know why I'm here. Stop acting like it's something else."

Persia unzipped her pants and pulled her dick out. She didn't bother to take off any clothes. She climbed between Ashli's legs and entered her without romance. Ashli didn't look at her or bother to move at all. She just laid back while Persia rocked back and forth on top of her. Persia choked Ashli and thrust harder and faster. Sweat beaded off Persia's forehead and dripped all over Ashli's face. Her breathing deepened in Ashli's ear.

"Oh my Go..." Ashli screamed. Her entire body convulsed between Persia and the bed. Persia increased her speed, and Ashli fought against her to stop. Ashli started convulsing again and screamed out before she fell limp. Persia pulled out of Ashli. She pulled a baby wipe off the dresser and cleaned herself off. She tucked herself back into her pants and zipped back up. Ashli didn't move.

"Next time." Persia left the room. Ashli curled up in the white duvet and listened for the sound of the front door closing.

"Next time, baby," Ashli whispered, smiled, and passed out.

CHAPTER SIX

"Your phone is ringing," Kevin yelled across the hotel room. Jas bounced out of the bathroom onto the bed. She smiled and answered the phone.

"Hey baby," she sang into the phone. Her legs swung in the air as she rolled around on the bed. "Yes, I will be home today, this evening. What do you want to do?"

"The wife?" Kevin asked. He pulled her across the bed and kissed, sucked her toes.

"Yes, it is. Baby, Kevin over here playing too much, I'm trying to talk to you." Jas giggled. "She said hi."

"Hi Shamia, how are you?" Kevin snatched the phone and walked into the bathroom to continue his conversation with Jasmyne's wife, Shamia. Jas waited patiently on the bed. She wasn't worried. Kevin returned and gave her the phone back. "Hey babe...dinner, huh."

"It's been a while since the three of us went out. I owe Shamia a date. Don't you think?" Kevin smiled at Jas.

"You are so right, Kevin. Baby, he needs to take us out. Wine and dine us. Where is the courting." Kevin's smile slowly turned into concern. He could tell Shamia was confirming Jas's statements by the look on her face. She was highly satisfied. This wasn't going exactly how he expected. Jas started laughing. "Ok, baby, I miss you. I can't wait to see you. Ok. See you in a minute."

"You thought you were going to say anything at all to my wife, and she wouldn't be on my side? Now, Kevin, I told you...you can try, but it won't work." Jas caressed Kevin's face and playfully slapped him. "Baby, as long as we stay in our lane and respect everyone else's lane...we will be ok."

"It's time for you to get out of here," Kevin said as he pushed Jas back into the bathroom. She laughed at him.

She peeked out of the bathroom, "When would you like me to add you to our calendar?"

Kevin was confused. He completely forgot about his throuple date he roped himself into. "Huh?"

"Pay attention and stay on your toes, and you won't have to say huh all the time." Jas shot Kevin a look. She gently encouraged him to embrace his royalty. She pushed him to act like a King and treat others as a King would. "You owe us a date."

"Tonight. You, me, and Shamia. I will pick you up at 8:30 pm," he responded. Kevin knew she was right; he trusted her. Jas helped him become a better man in his own eyes. She was able to see the man he truly was and never pushed her idea of who he should be on him. That meant a lot to him; he'd experienced too many women with the opposite mindset.

"Awe, aren't you sweet. Thank you. I know Shamia will be excited to see you." Jas was sincere in her response. She knew Kevin was trying to be a bit messy when he spoke to her wife, and she knew the date was her idea. She also knew he could have responded differently or declined.

The two left the hotel and headed to their separate destinations. Jas went home to her wife. Kevin turned towards his mother's house to pick up his son. He couldn't help wondering about a life with the four of them.

Instead, he decided to do something sweet for his wife. He knew she was at work today, so he made a quick turn and changed his direction. Maybe all Ashli needed was some romance to pull her back to him. Did he even want her to come back to him emotionally? He was sure there was nothing he could do to get her to leave physically, but it didn't stop him from thinking about it on the entire drive to her job.

"I'm here to see Ashli Jameson," Kevin stated to the gay gentleman sitting behind the counter, *probably the receptionist.*

"Um, do you have an appointment, sir?" the slender guy seated in front of him asked.

"I don't need an appointment. I'm not here for services. Ashli is my wife. I'm Kevin Jameson, her husband." Kevin answered. He was intrigued by the surprised look on the receptionist's face. As if he didn't know Ashli had a husband. He could be to blame for that. He never had a reason to come to her job.

"Ok, sir, take a seat, and I will get her for you." Shayne, his nametag read, walked Kevin to a small waiting room. It was very private. As he exited, he greeted the next person rather loudly, "Brian, how are you? I already know. Come with me!"

Ten minutes later, Ashli came rushing through the door. "What are you doing here?"

"I came to take you to lunch. We haven't spent much time together." Kevin pulled Ashli towards him.

"I am so busy today. I told you, I need to make appointments for everything...including lunch with you." She gave him a vague kiss on the cheek and headed towards the door. "I have a client waiting on me. I have to go, but when I see you tonight, we will plan something, ok?"

"Of course. I have a dinner meeting tonight, but I will see you at home afterward." He kissed Ashli on the forehead and walked out of the room in front of her. He didn't bother to say goodbye to Shayne, the receptionist, but Shayne made it a point to say goodbye to him.

"Bye-bye, Kevin, the husband!" Shayne yelled after Kevin as he left.

He had an uneasy feeling about the whole interaction. If this were 3 years ago, he probably would have gotten jealous and made a scene. Not this time. A small part of him hoped she was falling for someone else so she could release him. Kevin's mind raced as he walked through the parking lot and then sat in his car. Dinner plans with Jasmyne and Shamia were the highlight of his day. Ashli would be at work until this evening, and KJ was still with his grandmother. She fussed Kevin out if he picked KJ up before she called him. He needed something to do.

THREE HOURS LATER, Kevin woke up in his bed. He decided to come home to relax for a moment since Ashli and KJ were gone for the rest of the day. He was only supposed to lay on the bed for a moment. That moment turned into a much-needed nap. Kevin barely slept at home. He felt a need to stay on guard. He thought Ashli would never have done the things she has done. Now, there's no telling what she's really capable of.

"Aight, get up and get ready. You got your chance to relax." Kevin motivated himself to get moving. He jumped into the shower and rinsed away the negative feelings he was carrying from his interaction with Ashli. Something wasn't right with her, but he didn't have the time or the energy to figure it out.

He pulled a button-down shirt, jeans, and a blazer from the closet. He wasn't sure if the dress code required a blazer, so it was better to be prepared. Time flew by while he finished getting ready. He had made reservations for three earlier in the day, and two rose bouquets were waiting for him at the florist. As much as he enjoyed his time with Jas, he was quite intrigued by the trio's dynamic. Tonight was the night they took things to the next level. Shamia and Kevin rarely interacted. His phone rang, interrupting his thoughts.

"Hello," he answered.

"Kevin, how are you? I'm calling to confirm our plans for tonight." Shamia was very punctual. "Are you still picking us up at 8 pm?"

"I will see you on time," Kevin responded with pure happiness on his face.

"DINNER WAS AMAZING, Kevin. You outdid yourself this time." Shamia complimented Kevin as she brushed against him. He leaned back onto his car, and she followed.

The evening went smoothly. They enjoyed a late candle-lit dinner at their favorite spot, owned by a throuple. They provide an intimate environment customized for non-monogamous customers. Shamia enjoyed herself and showed her gratitude and attraction through physical touch. Jas gave the two a little space; it turned her on to see how much Shamia and Kevin were attracted to each other. She rested on the hood of the car.

"Are you two going to join me at my place tonight?" Jas asked, playfully interrupting the two lovers.

"As much as I would love to, Jas baby, I can't. I need to pick up KJ today from my mom's. She called me earlier today." It had been a few days since he'd seen KJ. "That means you will have to be back at work bright and early in the morning."

"Hmph. Ok." Jas pretended to pout and then hugged Kevin. She loved being KJ's nanny. It gave her the chance to spend time with him. "Back to the wife tonight?"

"If she's home. I doubt it. It may be a night for me and Junior." Kevin hugged Shamia and then kissed both ladies passionately. He opened their doors to allow them to get comfortable in his car. The ride home was comfortable. The ladies tried to convince Kevin to come home with them, but they knew it was pointless. Kevin's top priority was always his son. When he pulled up to their home, he walked them to the front door. They said their good nights, and Shamia went inside.

"Give me one moment; I will be in," Jas said to Shamia. She blew Jas a kiss before closing the front door. Jas redirected her attention to Kevin. "Are you going to be ok?"

"Jas baby, I'll be fine," Kevin reassured her.

"I'm worried about you," Jas held his face in her hands, forcing him to look her in the eyes. "A king can only carry so much."

In that moment, he knew he belonged with Jas, just as he had every time she had been there for him. He felt her looking into his soul, soothing the most vulnerable, hidden parts of him. She caressed him and cherished those parts of him. His wife used them as ammunition for her weapons against him; they were constantly at war.

"I love you." Kevin kissed Jas on the forehead. He thought of Jas his entire drive. His mother saw it in him again when he picked up KJ. He didn't fight her about it this time.

CHAPTER SEVEN

Three months rolled by like days. Jas continued to take care of KJ while Kevin and Ashli were at work. Although Jas had more than enough to prove Ashli wasn't at work as much as she said, she stopped indulging in conversations about it with Kevin. He had enough on his mind. Shamia, Jas, and Kevin continued to grow their relationship. They maintained their throuple date once every two weeks, while Jas and Kevin had their one-on-one dates on the opposite weeks. Kevin started to see himself building a life with both of them. While things were growing more and more positive with the throuple, Ashli was becoming less and less bearable. She was barely home, and when she was at home, all she did was sit on her phone. Her trips became more frequent. She was barely in town on the weekends anymore. Something had to give.

"Kevin!" Ashli yelled.

"What?" Kevin responded.

"I called your name maybe five times, and you didn't respond. What's going on with you?" Ashli faked concern. She was more annoyed at being ignored.

"I have a lot going on at work, that's all," he responded coldly.

"You are in I.T., don't act like you're some sort of exec with a lot of responsibilities," Ashli laughed. "I got a notification saying my phone bill is late. Did you pay for it?"

"No, I didn't. Don't you think it's time for you to start handling your own small bills? You've been at this job for almost two years and are always at work. That is your responsibility now." Kevin made sure to make direct eye contact with Ashli to enforce how serious he was. She glared at him, deciding if she wanted to fight this or not. Her glare slowly disappeared. He knew she wasn't going to fight it. There were too many secret doors that he could open when it came to her cell phone.

"Whatever, Kevin. You are such an asshole. You could have told me at the beginning of the month." She walked away, rolling her eyes. She let it go. He watched her snatch her wallet out of her purse on the couch and sit down. She pulled out a card he had never seen before and started typing on her phone. After a few moments, she smiled at him and walked back into the bedroom. He didn't know who paid the bill, but he knew for sure, she didn't.

THEIR RELATIONSHIP continued to move in the same direction. Ashli no longer asked Kevin for money at all unless it was a household bill. Kevin didn't offer to pay for anything extra for Ashli and didn't buy gifts like he used to. It seemed to make Ashli more irritated at Jas being in their home.

"Why are you qualified to be my son's nanny again?" Ashli sarcastically asked Jas.

"Ashli, let's not start this again. You know I have a master's degree in early childhood education. Are you okay?" Jas responded.

"I'm fine. I just don't understand why you are always in my house." Ashli cut her eyes at Jas.

"Well, someone has to be here to take care of YOUR son when Kevin is at work... and you're not here... so..." Jas shrugged her shoulders. "...that's why I have a full-time job."

"I'm home now, so you can go." Ashli waved Jas off towards the door.

"Ashli, the last time I left early because you were home...KJ ended up with the neighbor because you had to go. You know Kevin wants me to stay until he returns." Jas sat down on the couch next to KJ. She started tickling him, and he burst into laughter. Ashli's annoyance invaded her face. She was disgusted with how close KJ and Jas were. She didn't try to build a bond with KJ but didn't want her to build one with him either.

"KJ, come..." Ashli's command was interrupted by the sound of the front door. KJ jumped up and ran to meet his daddy. He couldn't contain his excitement. Kevin rushed through the door and swept KJ into his arms.

"How's my boy?" KJ hugged Kevin's neck as tight as his little arms would allow him.

"He was a perfect angel today," Jas responded to Kevin. He looked up at her with a light of joy in his eyes. As if he was coming home to his son and wife but his wife was Jas. "How was your day, Dad?"

"It was good. I finished a big project that has been weighing on me. Now I have some time to relax." Kevin kept his eyes on his son as he played with him but responded to Jas. He knew better than to let Ashli see the enjoyment he felt with Jas. "Thanks for asking."

"My pleasure, Kevin." Jas let a small smile slip through, and Ashli caught it. She swore something was going on between the two of them but couldn't push too hard, or her secrets would start falling out. Jas turned towards Ashli, "Well, it's time for me to go. Have a great evening."

Ashli faked a smile and shot a glare back at Jas. "You too."

"We will walk you to your car," Kevin said, and KJ agreed.

"Why, it's just in the driveway," Ashli asked. Kevin didn't respond; he just looked at Ashli. She turned around and headed towards the bedroom, "Whatever."

"Come on," Kevin, KJ, and Jas walked to her car. KJ jumped into her arms, hugged her, and kissed her on the cheek. He jumped down and ran into the house.

"Looks like your son wants you to have some private time with me," Jas teased.

"He's a great judge of character." Kevin laughed. "I'll see you tomorrow."

"Of course, you will. I would kiss you, but I'm sure she's watching." Jas looked past Kevin towards their bedroom window. She didn't see anyone, just the vertical blinds swinging back and forth. "I told you. I'll just give you a hug. I'll tell the wife you said hello."

"Thank you." Kevin hugged Jas quickly. If he stayed close to her too long, she wouldn't care what Ashli saw. He wouldn't be able to control himself. "Have a good night."

Jas got into her car and pulled off without hesitation. There was no point in lingering in a moment that was not for them. This was his moment. He watched her drive away until her car disappeared into the sea of darkness and headlights. It was time to make a change. He walked back into the house. He heard

Ashli in the bathroom. She sounded like she was vomiting. He contemplated asking her if she was okay. He wasn't sure if he was really concerned or not. If she died in his house, he would have to answer questions.

"Are you okay," he knocked on the bathroom door.

"I'm fine. Go away. I just ate something that didn't agree with me." Ashli yelled while shoving her face into the toilet bowl. "I'm fine."

"Okay. I'll leave you alone. I'm going to keep an ear out for you." Kevin didn't want to wake up to her lying on the bathroom floor dead. Or worse, he didn't want KJ to find her like that. She didn't respond, but the vomiting sounds stopped. He started KJ's bedtime routine. It was going to take at least an hour to get him in bed.

"Is he asleep?" Ashli peaked into KJ's bedroom, where Kevin and KJ lay in the bed together.

"Yes, he is," Kevin whispered.

"Can I talk to you?" Ashli asked.

"Sure, give me a minute to come out there," Kevin responded softly.

"What's up?"

I have to go see my mother for a few days. I didn't want to be gone for that long without letting you know." Ashli didn't bother to really look at Kevin. He knew she was lying. She never went to visit her mother. "I'm leaving tonight."

"Are you going to be okay on the road with the throwing up?" he asked her.

"Yeah, it's okay now. It stopped. I took something that will help," she responded.

"Be safe." Kevin turned around and went back into his son's room. He closed the door behind him without waiting for her to respond.

CHAPTER EIGHT

Brian sneaked up behind Ashli and wrapped his arms around her waist, resting his hands on her stomach where his child might grow one day. He caressed her stomach with his face nestled in her neck, inhaling her natural scent.

"Are you at it again?" Ashli laughed.

"You will be so beautiful carrying my child," Brian whispered in Ashli's ear. He wanted nothing more than to make them official and start a family. The ring was burning a hole in his pocket for three months since their trip to visit his family. He couldn't wait anymore. "...but I want to do this the right way."

Ashli couldn't have predicted Brian's next move, although, with all the signs she was throwing out, she should have. He stepped back away from her while pulling her body around to face him.

"Every minute I spend with you is another minute of pure happiness. I can't imagine living a moment of my life without you. When I met you, I was in the dark, and your beautiful smile has been my light ever since." Brian began his speech. Ashli quickly realized the next words he was going to say. A sharp pain started climbing up her stomach into her chest. She watched him reach into his pocket as he continued to speak. "I want you to help me build a home, mother our children..." It was as if a blade was inside her, and as he spoke, the blade grew larger and sharper. It reached her throat, and she couldn't stop Brian from continuing. "Ashli Jameson, will you make my dreams come true and be my wife?"

Brian was kneeling in front of Ashli. She rested her mouth in her hands to muffle the screams that never made it out. The blade was emerging from her throat, and all she could do was release it. Ashli bent over in front of Brian with his face lit up, waiting for an answer; she threw up all over his legs and the floor. His shock was minimal as he continued to wait for her answer. He knew she'd be able to speak now instead of speaking. Ashli grabbed a towel and ran into the bathroom. She collapsed on the floor in front of the toilet and made the toilet bowl her pillow. Anything that could reach up from her stomach through her throat was diving into the toilet, and she couldn't do anything to stop it. Brian didn't move. He stayed in the same spot on his one knee, soaked in vomit.

"I'm pregnant!" Ashli finally yelled out of the bathroom. "I don't know who it is."

Brian immediately snapped out of it and rushed to the bathroom. His pale skin was bright red with anger and sadness. "What did you say?"

"I'm sorry, Brian. I'm pregnant. I'm married. I have another boyfriend besides you. I don't know who the father is." Ashli returned her face to the toilet bowl. Tears fell from her face because of the physical pain she was feeling. She didn't feel any emotional pain for Brian. Or Kevin. She couldn't stop thinking about what Persia would say.

"How many?" Brian's face changed as if he was a different person. The joy he previously felt was replaced by betrayal. He didn't know what this other feeling was, but it didn't hurt. It made things clear. It was like putting a pair of magic glasses on a blind person; now, he could finally see. "How many!"

"Three..." Ashli continued to vomit. The pain was getting worse, and things didn't feel right. Something was seriously wrong. "Brian, baby, something is wrong. I need to go to the hospital."

Brian ignored Ashli's pleas. He wasn't sure if he wanted to help her. If he cared anymore about whether she lived or died. Everything he thought she was was a lie. He had spent the last year with a stranger. She was married. How did she keep a husband from him? The toilet no longer served as Ashli's pillow. Now she was in the middle of the bathroom floor, balled up, grunting out of pain.

"Brian, please. My phone. I will call. Please!" Ashli managed to release the begging between the pain. She could see Brian was lost in his head. She was alone. Her vomit quickly turned from food to stomach lining to blood. "Brian!!"

When she finally screamed, he focused on reality again. He picked her up into his arms and headed towards the front door, snatching up a blanket and her slides in the process. He put her in his back seat and headed towards the hospital. It wasn't the baby's fault. He couldn't let an innocent baby die because she was a heartless bitch. He pulled into the hospital emergency room driveway. He quickly jumped out of the car and ran around to the passenger side back door, where Ashli was attempting to slide herself out. She moved like she was pregnant for months but didn't show a physical sign of pregnancy.

"Help, somebody get out here and help!" he yelled towards the emergency room doors. Nurses rushed out with a gurney and started asking a lot of questions he didn't have the answers to. "I don't know. She just told me she was pregnant."

"Are you the father?" a nurse asked him. She was impatiently waiting for an answer he couldn't really provide.

"I don't know," he said shamefully, as if it was he who had nothing to be ashamed about. "I don't know, just help her."

"Sir, we will get her some help right now, but I need to ask you a few questions. Can you fill out some forms for us?" the nurse asked and directed him to the waiting room. An orderly walked up with a clipboard and forms. "Sir, can you fill out these forms."

"I'm not her husband," Brian whispered. The nurse seemed confused. "What? Can you say that again?" she asked him.

"I'm not her fucking husband. Here's her phone. Call her husband. His name is Kevin." Brian dropped the phone in the nurse's hands and stood up. "Fuck!"

"Sir, wait, please!" the nurse yelled at Brian's disappearing back as he walked out of the emergency room.

He got into his car and looked into his backseat. Blood, vomit, sweat. He sighed, turned back around, and stared at the street in front of him.

"Fuck her!" he pulled off.

CHAPTER NINE

The darkness muted any negative thoughts Kevin could drum up. He couldn't help but feel at ease while he held his sleeping son. KJ's little bed wasn't comfortable for a grown man, but it didn't matter. Any chance to be close to his son, Kevin took it. A vibration started on his thigh; it startled him. He had a call. 2 AM. Not answering. He slid the phone back into his pocket. Vibrations started again. Irritated, Kevin got out of his son's bed and answered the phone.

"Hello?" he said.

"Mr. Jameson? Can I speak to Mr. Jameson, please?" a young woman on the other end requested.

"This is Kevin Jameson. What is going on?" Kevin's emotions evolved from irritation to worry. *It's never a good thing when someone calls in the middle of the night and asks for you by your full name.*

"Mr. Jameson, this is Mercy General Hospital. Your wife came into the emergency room..." Before the young woman could finish her sentence, the questions started flying.

"Wait, what? My wife is where? She's not in town. She went to see her... Who brought her in? Is she okay?" Kevin's mind raced, and he couldn't contain himself.

"Mr. Jameson, Mr. Jameson. Please, Mr. Jameson. She is stable. We can give you all the details, but you need to come to the hospital. How long will it take you?" the young woman calmed him.

"I will be there in 30 minutes." Kevin hung up the phone, snatched clothes out of KJ's top drawer, and paused. There was no way he was going to take KJ to the emergency room this late. He made a call.

"...I don't know what's going on, but can you come watch KJ?" Kevin didn't remember going into the whole story, but Shamia was agreeing on the other end. She told him she would get dressed and be there in less than ten minutes. She said Jas would meet him at the hospital.

Everything was a blur until Kevin found himself standing in the emergency room. He hadn't asked anyone for help or even moved past the waiting room. He froze.

"Baby, what did they say?" Jas grabbed Kevin's arm, and he stared blankly at her. She caressed his face, "Kevin, are you there?"

He nodded his head. Yes. His eyes were still blank. Jas was worried about him; she had never seen him like that before. She attempted to comfort him to bring him back so they could find out what was going on with Ashli.

"Kevin, you have to snap out of it. We have to find out what's going on, and you're the only one that can do that." Jas slapped Kevin. They didn't have time for a breakdown.

"I'm here. I'm here." Kevin searched the ground around him frantically.

"He is still asleep at your house with Shamia," Jas answered the unasked questions.

"Thank you. Ok." Kevin walked towards the front desk. Jas felt better about his demeanor. He knew he would have to maintain himself. He couldn't let his fear show. There were too many women and his son that depended on him. "I'm here to see Ashli Jameson, my wife."

The nurse checked the information on the computer and walked them to another part of the hospital. A doctor sat down with them and explained Ashli was pregnant and she was having an adverse effect. They weren't sure why she was declining, but they were able to stabilize her.

"Can I see her?" Kevin asked.

"I will have a nurse show you where she is when she can have a visitor. Right now, we are just waiting," the doctor finished and quickly walked away.

"She's ok for now. Did you know she is pregnant?" Jas asked Kevin. His face answered before he could.

"No, I didn't know. We tried for so many years, and she never..." he dropped his head in his hands. Confusion was invading his mind. For years, they tried to have a child of their own, and nothing worked. When KJ came along, Kevin thought he would never have children. "She's not pregnant by me."

"I didn't... That's not why I asked Kevin." Jas was offended. She stepped back from him.

"I want you to know. I haven't slept with her in six months. There's no way she's pregnant with my child. Jasmyne, I don't want to keep stretching this out. I want you. I want you and Shamia. It's time for us to build our family." Kevin's face gleamed with clarity. "Don't say anything. Your wife is at my house right now taking care of my son. She didn't ask any questions at all. She knew I'd need you here with me, and she's needed there. Everything worth having isn't a struggle. We are worthy."

"Kevin, this isn't the time for this." Although she loved hearing him say those words, she didn't want it to come from tragedy. Kevin pulled her body into his. He wrapped one arm around her waist. Her heart raced, breathing quickened. "Don't do this now."

"I will make sure she is okay. I will call her family down here. I can't spend another minute like this. She's only staying with me to punish me. I'm done paying in my happiness." Kevin kissed Jas passionately. She felt something she'd never felt from him before. "I love you, Jasmyne. I am in love with you and Shamia. It's time for us to blend our families."

"Are you sure?" Jas held her excitement. It didn't feel like the right time. Part of her didn't believe him. "Wait. Let's get through today, and we will talk about it later."

"This isn't..." Kevin knew words wouldn't work. He reached into his pocket and pulled out a little blue box. "I didn't come to this decision lightly. You three are my family."

Kevin got down on one knee in the middle of the hallway in the hospital. He took a deep breath and cradled Jas's hand in his. He looked into her eyes and asked, "Jas, will you marry me?"

"Fuck you, Kevin!" Jas giggled. "Fuck you for making me so happy. Of course, I will."

Jas extended her arm, and he slid the ring on her finger.

"Hey...you know you have to ask Shamia too?" Kevin pulled another little blue box out of his pocket.

"The plan was to ask you both at the same time." Kevin smiled. He leaned in to hug her. Jas pushed him back.

"Nope, go see your wife." Jas pointed towards the nurse heading in their direction. Kevin looked at the nurse and back at Jas.

"Soon to be ex-wife," he whispered.

"Mr. Jameson?" the nurse asked.

"Yes, can I see her?" Kevin responded.

"Come with me," the nurse motioned for Kevin to follow her down the hallway. He disappeared from Jas's sight quickly. She sat down in the waiting room. Waiting was all she could do.

CHAPTER TEN

The streetlights were constant reminders he was still alive. It didn't feel like he was breathing anymore. Brian's heart felt like it was out of his chest. Ashli was one of the lowest beings he had ever encountered. He couldn't believe he thought they were in love. He forgot the ring was still in his pocket until the box started stabbing his thigh.

"Fuck, fuck fuck!" Brian yelled to himself. His car protected the rest of the world from his pain, expressed verbally. Sweat continued to pour down his head and back. "Fuck!"

Brian made a u-turn and headed back to the hospital. There was still a small chance the child was his, and he couldn't let them die alone in the hospital. He pulled into the emergency room driveway without parking, and he rushed into the hospital.

"Ashli Jameson, what room is she in?" Brian asked the nurse. She asked about his relationship, and he lied, "I'm her brother."

He frantically moved through the hospital hallways, looking for her room. As he approached her room, Kevin walked out. He looked directly at Brian; he remembered him.

"Hey, I'm Kevin. You're here to see Ashli?" he asked Brian.

"Yeah, I was just checking on her." Brian lied. Kevin surveyed Brian's face for signs of emotion. He had a feeling this guy standing in front of him with bloodshot eyes and a pale complexion was one of Ashli's lovers. He shook Brian's hand.

"She's pregnant. It's not mine. I'm assuming it's yours?" Kevin didn't have time for formalities. He knew exactly what he wanted for the rest of his life, and all this was in the way. Brian hesitated to respond, but he wasn't going to back down.

"Well..." Before Brian could start, a young, black, masculine woman was rushing down the hallway straight for them. It was the brown-skinned, beautiful, curvaceous woman with her that caught their attention.

"Excuse me," Kevin stood in front of the hospital room door as the masculine woman attempted to rush past them. "How can I help you?"

"My apologies, man. My name is Persia. Nice to finally meet you." Persia reached out for a handshake that never showed up. She looked at Brian's confused face and back at Kevin. "Is there a problem?"

"How do you know Ashli?" Kevin asked.

"Her and I have interacted for a while." Persia stepped back in defense. It didn't seem like Kevin knew about her. "She told me you knew."

"Yeah, that sounds about right," Kevin laughed. He pointed towards Brian,

"You're her girlfriend; this is her boyfriend, Brian."

"Damn. She told me you knew her about me." Persia glanced at the woman next to her. "Lexi, it's time for us to go."

"Do you want to check in on her?" Kevin asked. He was unusually calm to be a husband standing with his wife's female and male lovers. "She must have called you, right?"

"No, the hospital called me. They found my number in her family contacts on her phone." Persia slipped her hand into Lexi's. "We don't have time for drama. Just let her know I came to check on her. She's okay?"

"She's okay for now. She's stable and improving," Kevin answered, looking at Brian. He seemed to be the most concerned out of them all. His eyes were about to overflow with tears. "Brian, you can go see her. I'm leaving, too."

Persia turned around without speaking and started walking away with Lexi until she stopped in her tracks.

"Are you just going to leave her here like that?" Lexi asked Persia. "Is that how we treat people?"

"No, it's not. I'm not her husband or her boyfriend. We had a sexual relationship, but after this. It's time for us to move forward and leave all this behind us." Persia responded, caressing Lexi's face. "I have someone I want you to meet."

Lexi felt a blind date coming on. Persia was adamant about finding their third partner. She started walking again, signaling Persia to follow. "Okay, let's go."

Persia and Lexi disappeared on the elevator, and Brian watched them. Kevin could see the pain on Brian's face. He remembered a time when he was carrying that same pain. He wasn't willing to carry that baggage anymore. He decided to set all that down right there in the hospital hallways. He headed back into Ashli's room and left Brian.

"Ashli, can you hear me?" Kevin spoke softly next to Ashli's bed.

"Yes," she responded.

"Brian is right outside. He is going to come in and stay with you after I leave." Kevin began.

"Leave?" Ashli whispered. "It's Jas, right?"

"I know about Brian and Persia. He's your child's father; I know I'm not. I don't need to know anymore," Kevin continued.

"I don't know who the baby's father is," Ashli whispered, tears fell from her face.

"There's more?" Kevin stopped himself. He didn't want to know the details. "I will make sure you are taken care of in the divorce. I'll pay for school. You can keep the house; KJ and I are moving out. No, it isn't about Jas, but yes, she and I have started a relationship."

"This wasn't the time for that," Brian stated in the room doorway. Ashli looked over at him and then back at Kevin. She knew her house of cards had already come down. "She's not well. It's probably a good idea for you to go."

Kevin smiled at Brian. "You're right. It's time for me to go. Good luck."

Kevin walked out the hospital room door without looking back. He pulled his phone out of his pocket and dialed Jas. "Meet me out front. It's time for us to go."

Brian sat down next to Ashli's bed, "How are you feeling?"

"I have to tell you something," Ashli continued to cry.

"I know about them both. It's okay. We will figure this out. I told you, I love you. All you have to do is be honest with me." Brian held Ashli's hand. He finally felt they would get a sincere chance at love. Ashli pulled her hand out of his.

"There's one more thing. The baby still might not be yours," Ashli looked away from Brian.

"I did the calculation; it happened when we went to see my family." Brian allowed a bit of joy to show on his face. He wanted Ashli to agree with him.

Let them move forward with their family. He knew she wouldn't let that happen.

"Brian, there was someone else. He may be the father." Ashli couldn't let any more lies fester. She was sure all the medical issues she was experiencing were her lies manifesting themselves into her body. "I can tell you if you want to know."

Brian sat with his head resting in his hands with a slight shiver over his entire body. It wasn't cold, he felt, but an abundance of pain and anger. He didn't move. He couldn't speak.

"Brian, maybe you should wait until I have the paternity test. We can finish this talk then." She knew this was a hard pill to swallow, and he wasn't going to be able to take the full truth. She stopped their conversation there.

"Look." Brian sat up, resting her hand between his. "If nothing else, I'm still your friend. I'm here for you. We will talk about everything else after the paternity test. I don't want to hear anymore. But it's okay."

"Thank you, Brian. Thank you." This was the first time Ashli had someone who would stay with her no matter what. Her husband loved her, but his love had conditions; Brian's didn't. "I hope this baby is yours."

"Me too," he whispered, kissing her hand.

CHAPTER ELEVEN

Kevin and Jas walked into his house to meet Shamia and KJ. Jas was intertwined on Kevin's arm with excitement highlighting her face. Kevin told Jas everything about Brian, Persia, and the mystery man. She couldn't believe it. Everything finally made sense. She was ecstatic about telling her wife about their next step in life. The ring shined on Jasmyne's finger. Shamia knew it was coming and patiently waited for Kevin to figure it out for himself.

"Shamia, KJ?" Jas called through the house. KJ came running out of his room and jumped into Jas's arms. Shamia followed behind him. "Hey, little man."

"Shamia, Jas, and I need to speak to you." Shamia read Jas's face and glanced at her finger.

"Kevin, I think you need to hear the message on your answering machine. Who has answering machines anymore?" Shamia walked over to the machine and pressed play.

"Ashli, this is Robert, Robert Schultz. I got a call from the hospital; I tried your cell phone, but no one answered. I just want to make sure you are ok. Is the baby okay?" a man's voice echoed throughout the house. Kevin's face had confusion written all over it. *Same last name as Brian.*

"That must be the mystery man," Jas said to Kevin. He shook a chuckle off and released the last bit of negativity linked with Ashli. He walked over to the two women and held their hands in his. Shamia and Jas held hands, forming a triangle between the three. "Jasmyne and Shamia, will you commit yourselves to me and allow me to commit myself to only you two?" "Well, it's about time. I didn't think you would ever see what you had right in front of you," Shamia giggled. "Jas?"

"I love you both," Jas's smile lit up, and she threw her hand up. "I gave my answer."

"Me?" KJ stood in the middle of the triangle, looking up at them.

"I love you all, your dad, Jasmyne, and you KJ. We are a family now," Shamia responded. He looked at his dad and then at Shamia. He remembered the love from them all and smiled.

"K," he responded. He hugged each of them around their legs. The three of them moved closer into the middle into one big hug. Shamia pulled back just a bit.

"And the rings?" she asked. All three of them laughed; KJ joined in with no idea what he was laughing at. Kevin reached into his pocket and pulled out the small box identical to the one he had earlier.

"Will this do?" he asked Shamia, opening the box. She allowed a small smile to break through.

"It will do, for now." She slid the ring on her finger and admired it. Both the ladies held their ring fingers in the air. Two rings rested on each of their ring fingers. "Now it's time to replace that ring on your finger."

Shamia grabbed Kevin's hand and took his wedding band off.

EPILOGUE

Ashli quickly recovered from her illness. The doctors could not pinpoint a cause but leaned towards stress. She completed a paternity test that proved her baby was Brian's child. The morning-after pill didn't work. After seeing how Brian stood by her and protected her from her husband, she decided to say yes to his question. Before they could move forward in honesty, she had to reveal the identity of her third lover. Robert Schultz left a message on Ashli's answering machine and confirmed he received a call just as the rest of Ashli's lovers did. Ashli did have an affair with Brian's father, Robert. It happened before she realized he was related to Brian. When she saw him the weekend she met Brian's family, she was disgusted and cut it off with him. She explained everything to Brian. He told her she needed to go to therapy, but he wouldn't leave her. She had a little girl and married Brian.

Jasmyne, Shamia, Kevin, and KJ moved into a new home together. Their joint income opened a new level of opportunity for them. They opened multiple businesses, helping keep jobs in their neighborhood. It took no time for Jasmyne to get pregnant with all the love in their home. Jasmyne continued to take care of KJ during the day while Shamia and Kevin went to work.

She enjoyed being a stay-at-home mom. Kevin's mom met Jas and Shamia, and as long as her son was genuinely happy, she welcomed them with open arms.

Kevin kept his word in his divorce. He paid for Ashli to finish school, paid off the house, and gave it to her. He let her keep everything in the house and her car. She also received alimony until she married Brian. Kevin and Ashli never spoke again after their divorce was final. She didn't attempt to apologize or acknowledge anything she did in their marriage. Kevin was happy to be in a place that he didn't need her to.

Persia and Ashli didn't have sex after that. Persia didn't feel comfortable with the amount of deceit that was going around. She had to remove herself.

They maintained a friendship from a distance; Brian was okay with it. Persia and Lexi...well, I guess you will have to read Chocolate Obsession to find out what happens with Persia and Lexi.

Don't miss out!

Visit the website below and you can sign up to receive emails whenever Shaun J. Phree publishes a new book. There's no charge and no obligation.

https://books2read.com/r/B-A-VVFM-XODJB

BOOKS 2 READ

Connecting independent readers to independent writers.

Did you love *Vanilla Fetish*? Then you should read *C. Obsession*[1] by Shaun J. Phree!

[2]

In this tantalizing conclusion to the "Chocolate Caramel Vanilla" series, Persia's journey of passion and peril reaches its climax. Reeling from the loss of two of her lovers, Persia stands at a crossroads, her heart torn between past affections and a burgeoning romance with Lexi, whose enigmatic allure captivates and confounds.

---

1. https://books2read.com/u/3y6JJJ

2. https://books2read.com/u/3y6JJJ